PUFFIN BOOKS

# Hamster and a Robbery

Elizabeth Hawkins lives in London and Dorset. She has written a number of books for children of all ages and she also teaches and lectures on writing for children.

*Some other books by Elizabeth Hawkins*

A MONSTER OF A HAMSTER
HAMSTER IN DANGER

Elizabeth Hawkins

# Hamster and a Robbery

*Illustrated by Ben Cort*

PUFFIN BOOKS

*To the children of*
*Devonshire Hill School, Tottenham*

PUFFIN BOOKS

Penguin Books Ltd, 27 Wrights Lane, London W8 5TZ, England
Penguin Putnam Inc., 375 Hudson Street, New York, New York 10014, USA
Penguin Books Australia Ltd, Ringwood, Victoria, Australia
Penguin Books Canada Ltd, 10 Alcorn Avenue, Toronto, Ontario, Canada M4V 3B2
Penguin Books India (P) Ltd, 11 Community Centre, Panchsheel Park, New Delhi – 110 017, India
Penguin Books (NZ) Ltd, Cnr Rosedale and Airborne Roads, Albany, Auckland, New Zealand
Penguin Books (South Africa) (Pty) Ltd, 5 Watkins Street, Denver Ext 4, Johannesburg 2094, South Africa

On the World Wide Web at: www.penguin.com

Penguin Books Ltd, Registered Offices: Harmondsworth, Middlesex, England

First published 2001
1


Made and printed in England by Clays Ltd, St Ives plc



British Library Cataloguing in Publication Data
A CIP catalogue record for this book is available from the British Library

ISBN 0-141-31011-1

# Contents

# 1. An Important Announcement

Class 3 of Hopswood Junior School stood in line to go in to assembly. At the front, Anna-Louise's red curls twisted back and forth as she peered along the line.

'Where's Luke? He didn't walk to school with me today.'

'Stop talking now,' boomed Mr Pigott, their class teacher, who always shouted too loud. 'There is to be an important announcement in assembly today, and we mustn't be late.'

'But Luke might be lost or kidnapped or squashed by a runaway bus,' said Anna-Louise.

Luke ducked down behind Ali at the end of the line.

He'd been doing his best to keep away from Anna-Louise because whenever she was around Luke always seemed to get into trouble.

An elbow dug into Luke's ribs.

'I'm watching the second episode of *Murder in the Marsh* on telly tonight,' whispered Ali. 'What did you think of the first?'

'Mum wouldn't let me watch,' said Luke. 'What's it about?'

'Mega scary! People get pulled into

the marsh and sucked into this sinking mud . . .'

'Is there talking still at the back,' boomed the approaching voice of Mr Pigott. 'Who is that skulking at the back? Luke! I might have known.' Mr Pigott's eyebrows twitched fiercely.

'Anna-Louise is worried about you, Luke. I think you'd better go and stand at the front next to her where I can keep an eye on you.'

Luke scowled at Anna-Louise as together they led the class into assembly.

The headteacher, Mrs Harrington, rose from her big chair and beamed down from the platform.

'Tomorrow, children,' she began, 'the school inspectors are to visit us. What a pleasure it will be to welcome them to Hopswood Junior School to see our good work.'

'They're not going to read my stories, are they, Luke?' whispered Anna-Louise anxiously. 'I'm no good at stories.'

Mrs Harrington's grey eyes searched the hall, and seemed to linger on Luke and Anna-Louise.

'And you, children,' continued Mrs Harrington, 'will be as helpful, hard-working and as well behaved as usual. Each classroom will be tidy. Rubbish will be in the bin. Broken furniture and equipment will be left in the corridor for Mr Tump the caretaker to collect.'

Mrs Harrington's smile swept over the children like a chilling wave. 'And I am sure we will pass this inspection with flying colours.'

She picked up her big black handbag and marched out of the hall.

'Look at Mrs Harrington's chair,' said Samantha, giggling. 'She's not going to pass, is she?'

It was true. As Luke filed past Mrs Harrington's chair, he saw tufts of white stuffing bursting out of a small hole in the leather seat.

'Are they inspecting her too?' said Luke with surprise.

'Yeah,' said Ali, who had pushed through to look. 'It's like those inspectors on telly. Not the ones in uniform, the important ones in raincoats. They suspect everybody. They spy on people, tap telephones, carry handcuffs . . . You can end up in prison.'

'No!' Anna-Louise's hand clapped over her open mouth.

## 2. A Cleaning Crisis

There was reading, writing and number work as usual in Class 3 that morning. After school lunch, Class 3 often had interesting activities like art or football or gardening, but not today.

'Class 3 must look immaculate before you all go home,' boomed Mr Pigott.

Samantha collected up all the chewed and slimy rubbers. Ali tidied up the rough-paper cupboard. The twins, David and Delia, bossed everyone around.

'Luke, throw out those old twigs on the windowsill,' said David.

'And you'd better wash that green mould out of the jam jar too,' ordered Delia.

'And Luke,' shouted Mr Pigott, 'straighten those drawings on the wall above your table.'

Luke rushed around panting.

'What about Anna-Louise?' he said. 'Why isn't she helping? She can put the drawings straight.'

Anna-Louise stood there, wringing her hands, her face pale with fear.

'I don't know what to do,' she wailed. 'If the inspectors don't like my stories, will I go to prison?'

'Yes,' said Delia, grinning. 'In handcuffs, for ever and ever.'

'Handcuffs, prison. Dreadful things you children talk about,' said Mr Pigott, flapping about, his arms waving in the air. 'You children watch far too much television. Now, Anna-Louise, *make yourself useful.*'

'I don't know . . .'

'Yes you do,' declared Mr Pigott. 'When did we last clean the hamster's cage out?'

'Ooh,' said Samantha, wrinkling her nose. 'It's all smelly.'

'Luke and I cleaned it out last week,' said Ali. 'And it's not my turn. I'm not cleaning out that stinky cage again.'

Mr Pigott lifted the cage with a flourish and wrinkled up his nose.

'Uhm! The inspectors won't like this

at all,' he said. 'There you are, Anna-Louise. Take the cage out to the bin by the back door and throw out all the dirty straw and sawdust, and put in fresh from the box outside.'

The smelly cage landed in Anna-Louise's arms.

'But I can't,' she protested, 'by myself. Who will hold the ham –'

'Anna-Louise!' Mr Pigott growled. 'We're all working hard. We're all doing our bit to keep the inspectors happy, and do you help? Do you think of the good of the class? Do you consider. . . ?'

Mr Pigott's voice rose in a squawk and his arms flapped more wildly.

Anna-Louise lugged the cage away as fast as she could. Mr Pigott was getting into quite a state about these inspectors. Perhaps the inspectors could put him in prison too.

'Luke,' she pleaded as she puffed past him, 'come and help me.'

'No, definitely not!' said Luke. 'Ali and I cleaned out the cage last week.'

'But how can I do it without anyone to help me,' pleaded Anna-Louise. 'Who'll hold the hamster?'

'I'm not listening,' Luke said, 'so you can stop asking. Every time you ask me to help with the hamster I get into big trouble and everyone blames me.'

*

Mr Pigott looked down at his watch.

'Where's Anna-Louise? She's been away a long time. Luke, that drawing of Samantha's . . . you've pinned it upside down.'

'I thought that was the right way up,' said Luke.

'What a *very* silly thing to do, Luke. If I can't trust you to pin the drawings the right way up, you had better go and find Anna-Louise.

Samantha sniffed as Luke walked past.

It was a relief to get out of the mad panic of the classroom into the cool, dark corridor to the back door. Luke had to climb over the broken tables and chairs left out for Mr Tump. It was a bit like an obstacle race.

Luke found Anna-Louise sitting by

the dustbins. In the cage was fresh sawdust, clean hay and sparkling water in the drip-feed bottle.

'Mr Pigott sent me to fetch you. I'll help you carry the cage . . . What's the matter with you?'

Anna-Louise's green eyes were bright with tears.

'Oh, Luke!' Anna-Louise moaned. 'I tried to tip out the smelly sawdust, but the hamster kept sliding around.' Sniff, sniff. 'I had to take him

out and put him down while I cleaned the cage. I put in fresh hay so the hamster could nest.' Sniff, sniff. 'I filled up the water.'

Luke's eyes widened with horror.

'What are you saying, Anna-Louise? *Where* did you put the hamster down?'

'In Mrs Harrington's chair.'

'In Mrs Harrington's chair?' demanded Luke.

'The big chair she sits on in assembly,' said Anna-Louise, sniffing.

'The one with the hole in the seat and the stuffing popping out?' asked Luke suspiciously.

'Yes. It was waiting in the corridor and the hole was just the right size for a hamster to snuggle in while his cage was being cleaned.'

Luke's heart was beating so hard he

was sure he could hear it. He looked back along the corridor. He couldn't see the chair. He looked in the cage too, but he couldn't see the hamster either.

'Where's the chair?' he demanded.

The tears tipped out of Anna-Louise's green eyes and chased down the freckles on her face.

'I think it's gone to be mended . . . Someone came and moved things . . . I didn't see. I was busy cleaning the cage.'

Luke took a deep breath. 'I'll carry the cage back. Mr Pigott is probably too busy to check on the hamster. You'll have to find the hamster before the inspectors come tomorrow.'

'All by myself?'

'Yes, all by yourself!'

# 3. A Cosy Trap

'Luke, I'm going to tell Mr Pigott,' said Anna-Louise in a quavery voice when they were back in the classroom.

'Do what you like. It's not my problem.'

Luke was determined to stay out of trouble and helping Anna-Louise always meant trouble.

Luke knew because he had lived next

door to Anna-Louise all his life.

Anna-Louise never pinched people, or borrowed things without asking, or said unkind things about other children. This was odd enough, but oddest of all, despite all this goodness, Anna-Louise was always getting into trouble and getting Luke into trouble too.

Luke and Anna-Louise set the hamster cage down on its table at the back of the class. Anna-Louise pushed her way through the busy children towards Mr Pigott.

'Mr Pigott, Mr Pigott,' she said.

'Cage cleaned out is it then?'

'Yes, Mr Pigott, but . . .'

'I don't want to hear any buts. Everyone is working hard to make the classroom presentable. If a job is worth doing, it's worth doing well, without any buts.'

'The hamster . . . he's . . . he's . . .' Anna-Louise's voice trembled.

'Anna-Louise, can't you see I'm busy?' Mr Pigott's teeth flashed white in his scraggy beard. 'If everyone made such a fuss over a little job, this classroom would never be ready. Now go and help Delia tidy the class library and I don't want to hear another word from you.'

At mid-afternoon break, Luke kicked a ball around the playground with Ali and David. Out of the corner of one eye he watched Anna-Louise lurking along the side of the playground wall. She was creeping towards the caretaker's house in the corner of the playground.

No wonder she kept looking back

nervously over her shoulder! Ever since some of the bigger boys had broken a window with a football, Mr Tump's house had been strictly out of bounds.

Luke kicked the ball away and spied on Anna-Louise over his shoulder.

She reached the front of the house and clasped the window sill. Slowly she pulled herself up, until she could see through the window. Then she fell. She screamed and stared at the blood-red trickles seeping out of her knees.

Luke ran as fast as he could and dragged her back into the main playground. Anna-Louise would be in real trouble if any of the teachers saw what she had been up to.

'Are you all right, Anna-Louise?'

'Luke, he's got Mrs Harrington's chair in there and he's already ripped the old leather off the seat.'

Luke turned as heavy steps approached behind.

'Anna-Louise!' said Mr Pigott. 'Was that you screaming? Oh dear, look at those knees. You'd better go to the school nurse and get a plaster on those grazes.'

Samantha took Anna-Louise to the nurse, while Mr Pigott stroked his beard and surveyed Luke.

'I saw you dragging Anna-Louise,' he said at last.

'I was helping her up,' said Luke.

'No, you weren't,' said Mr Pigott. 'You were dragging her along the ground. It looked very much like bullying to me.'

There was a sudden clanging behind him. The twins had crept up with the break bell and were ringing it loudly.

'We'd better get on tidying the classroom,' said Delia, blinking her big, baby blue eyes.

'There's not much of the school day left,' added David, shaking his shiny, blond hair.

'Thank you, David and Delia,' said Mr Pigott with a smile.

Luke followed the class inside.

It wasn't fair! Why was he always in trouble?

David and Delia, with their big, blue eyes and wide smiles looked so innocent that no grown up would believe the terrible behaviour they were capable of.

After school, Anna-Louise was waiting for Luke at the school gate. She had two pink plasters on each knee.

'The hamster is in the chair in Mr Tump's workshop. I'm sure he is,' Anna-Louise whispered urgently.

'Mr Tump will find him then,' said Luke casually.

'But Mr Tump won't find the hamster,' wailed Anna-Louise, running to keep up with Luke. 'The hamster was tired out with sliding all over his cage. He likes to nest and sleep in the day. He snuggled down so deep in the hole of Mrs Harrington's chair, Mr Tump will never notice him.'

'So?'

'So . . . if Mr Tump nails a new piece of leather on the seat, the hamster will be trapped inside. He won't like being sat on in assembly,' moaned Anna-Louise. 'And he's got such sharp teeth, they could easily bite through leather.

He might bite . . .'

'Bite Mrs Harrington's bottom,' Luke gasped.

In his mind he saw it all. Mrs Harrington, in her best iron-grey suit, leaping high in the air with a scream while the shocked inspectors looked on.

The local papers might hear about it . . . and Hopswood Junior School's name would be mud. Mud . . .

'I know,' said Luke quickly. 'I'll call round for you after tea. It's the second episode of *Murder in the Marsh* tonight.'

# 4. To the Rescue

'Mum, can I watch *Murder in the Marsh*?' said Luke as he finished his burger.

His mother sighed and put down her mug of tea.

'Luke, we had a big argument about that last week. These stories about horrible murders are not suitable for children. I've written to the television company to complain. There's too much violence . . .'

'OK,' said Luke.

Luke's father looked up from his paper with surprise.

'I'm glad you're seeing sense, son,' he said. 'Your mother's right.'

'I'll take my football out then,' said Luke.

'Half an hour,' said his mother, smiling.

Luke pulled on his trainers and was halfway down the garden path when the door opened.

'Heh! Luke!' called his dad, throwing something down the path. 'You forgot your new Liverpool FC football Uncle Paul sent you.'

Anna-Louise's shiny green door was opened by her mother in fluffy pink slippers. Her gaze dropped straight to Luke's trainers.

'Dirty shoes, Luke. I'm surprised your mother tolerates it. No, you're not coming into my kitchen in those filthy sports shoes. Wait here.'

Luke was never allowed in Anna-Louise's kitchen. It was the sort of kitchen you were only allowed to walk around in your socks, in case you made the floors dirty.

'Anna-Louise,' shrieked her mother. 'Luke has come to collect you for that programme on marsh wildlife.'

She turned back to Luke with a hint of a smile.

'I'm glad to hear you are interested in something other than football these days, Luke. Marsh wildlife should be very educational. I would watch with you, but I have my evening class at the

Institute. What have you got that football for?'

As Luke and Anna-Louise passed Luke's house, Luke dropped his new football carefully inside the front gate. Anna-Louise began walking up the path to Luke's front door.

'Where do you think you're going?' said Luke.

'I thought we were going to watch *Murder in the Marsh*.'

'Of course we're not,' said Luke. 'Mum would never let me watch it. We're going to get the hamster.'

'Oh, Luke!' said Anna-Louise. 'What a brilliant idea!'

'But this is the last time, ever,' muttered Luke. 'We've got to be quick. I've only got half an hour.'

They ran all the way to the school gates.

Too late – the gates were locked.

'We'll have to climb over,' said Luke.

He climbed up on the KEEP OUT – PRIVATE PROPERTY sign. Then he hauled himself up to the HOPSWOOD JUNIOR SCHOOL – HEADTEACHER: MRS HARRINGTON; CARETAKER: MR TUMP sign.

'Come on, Anna-Louise. Put your toes on MRS HARRINGTON.'

'Climbing makes me dizzy,' Anna-Louise gasped. 'I don't like heights.'

'I can't do this without you,' said Luke. 'Only you know where the hamster is.'

'I'll . . . I'll try,' said Anna-Louise fearfully, reaching up for Luke's hand.

Luke guided Anna-Louise over the

top and down the other side of the gate. They crept along the playground wall until they came to Mr Tump's house.

'Look,' whispered Anna-Louise. 'Mr Tump's left the door open.'

'He's probably emptying the rubbish bins in school,' said Luke.

They went through the door and found themselves in a workroom with tools hanging on the walls, ladders in one corner, and a lawnmower in another.

In the middle of the room stood a magnificent chair. The wooden arms and back gleamed with fresh polish, while the seat was thickly covered with plumb velvet.

'It's Mrs Harrington's chair. Isn't it beautiful?' sighed Anna-Louise. 'Don't you think that velvet is much nicer than leather?'

'But where's the hamster?' demanded Luke. 'Show me where you put him.'

Anna-Louise advanced on the chair with a puzzled expression. She pointed to a spot in the middle of the plum velvet.

'He was there, sort of.' She prodded around with her fingers. 'I can't feel him.'

'Here, let me try.'

Luke gave the chair seat a gentle poke.

'Ow!' He leaped in the air. 'He's in there. He bit me. Look, there's a tiny rip in the seat.'

'Don't spoil the seat, Luke. We'll have to lift the tacks pinning the velvet down on the sides of the seat, then we can lift the cover off.'

Luke lifted down two screwdrivers from the wall and they worked away on each side of the seat. It took ages before the first tack fell out.

Luke looked at his watch. 'I've got to be home in ten minutes. There must be at least ten tacks each side. At this rate we'll never get the velvet off.'

From outside came the rumble of wheels as a big rubbish bin was pushed across the playground.

'Mr Tump!' cried Anna-Louise.

'Quick, we've got to get out of here,'

said Luke. As he reached up to put the screwdrivers back on their wall hooks, he noticed a row of keys, hanging on hooks, each with its own label, behind the door.

'Push up the chair over here,' ordered Luke.

They dragged the chair over. Luke clambered up and stood very carefully on the wooden sides around the plum seat. He lifted off the key marked FRONT GATE.

'You take one side of the chair and I'll take the other,' he said.

Mr Tump suddenly stopped as he wheeled out one of the rubbish bins. He was sure he had heard someone open the front gate. He didn't have his glasses on, but . . . he blinked. Was that two figures carrying something bulky out along the road?

He left the wheely bin, and ran puffing into his workroom. Mrs Harrington's chair, which he had just spent hours glueing and polishing and covering with a beautiful bit of velvet cut from an old curtain, had gone.

Mr Tump pulled his phone from the pocket of his overalls and dialled.

'Is that Hopswood Police Station?' he said.

# 5. 'I'm Not a Robber!'

Luke lifted up the front legs and Anna-Louise took hold of the back of the chair. It was heavy and an awkward shape to carry.

'It's slipping, I can't hold it,' Anna-Louise gasped as she stumbled along the road.

'Put it down. We'll have a rest.'

They set the chair down and perched

side by side on the edge of the seat.

'The hamster must be asleep,' said Anna-Louise. 'My cousin is a baby and she's always crying, but when she's pushed round in her pram she sleeps. She likes the movement, you see. I expect hamsters . . .'

'Listen to that din,' said Luke, who wasn't particularly interested in babies. 'That's a siren, and it's coming our way.'

'Must be an ambulance,' said Anna-Louise.

'Or a fire engine,' said Luke.

But they were both wrong. A shining white police car with a flashing red light and strident siren rushed past them, up to the school gates . . . and then came back.

Luke was delighted that the police car

stopped right beside them. It looked like a new model. Yes! It was the new XK400 series B, with the latest roof-mounted search lights and the new, super-powerful siren.

The bulletproof window wound smoothly down at the touch of a button and a police officer with a neat, black moustache leaned out.

'You kids from Hopswood Junior School?'

'Yes,' said Luke helpfully.

'The gates are locked. Is there a side entrance open we can use?'

'I don't think so,' said Luke uncertainly.

'You can climb over the gates,' said Anna-Louise. 'We . . .'

Luke pinched Anna-Louise hard.

'You'll have to telephone Mr Tump,' said Luke quickly. 'He has the key.'

Luke felt a hot blush spreading up over his face. He put his hand in his pocket. He had the key!

'Mr Tump, the caretaker? We've spoken to him. There's been a robbery and they've made off with the key to the front gate. Sorry you can't help. Sometimes kids know other ways into school.'

With a zoom, the white car sped away, light flashing and siren shrieking.

'Isn't that awful?' said Anna-Louise as she picked up the back legs of the chair again. 'Mummy won't like that. It's so scary, robbers breaking into school . . .'

'Anna-Louise, don't be stupid, we're the robbers.'

The chair bumped to the ground as Anna-Louise let go of the legs. Her mouth dropped open in a round O.

'Mr Tump must have seen Mrs Harrington's chair had gone. He's called up the police station.'

'I'm not a robber, Luke,' wailed Anna-Louise. 'I know I'm not a robber.'

The hot blush faded from Luke's face. His face felt cold and clammy. He had to think . . . and fast.

'We'll have to put the chair somewhere out of sight while we get the hamster out. Can we hide it in your garden shed? Ours is crammed with stuff. Yours is always tidy.'

In Anna-Louise's garden shed, forks and spades hung neatly on walls. The wheelbarrow was tilted upright and even Anna-Louise and her father's bikes had a special wall-mounted rack. There was masses of room for a big, old chair.

'We can't,' cried Anna-Louise. 'When Mummy comes back from her evening class, she leaves her bag of tools in the shed.'

'Her tools? For cake decorating?'

'She's finished the cake-decorating class. Now she's in the furniture upholstery class.'

Luke frowned. Anna-Louise's shed would be too dangerous.

'We'll have to try and squeeze the chair into our shed,' he said doubtfully.

They struggled along as best they could with the chair bumping against their legs. As they rounded the corner into their road, Luke's heart sank.

There were the twins, Delia and David, sitting on a wall, playing with their yo-yos.

'Wasn't *Murder in the Marsh* terrifying?' said Delia grinning. 'I liked the bit where the lady in high heels and the fur hat was dropped over the bridge into the marsh mud.'

'Didn't you love the sucking, gooey, sticky sound of the mud?' said David. 'Is she the second or third victim of the marsh thieves, Luke?'

'Uhm, I can't remember,' said Luke.

'Of course he can't,' began Anna-Louise. 'His mother won't let . . .'

'That looks a bit like Mrs Harrington's chair,' said Delia.

'Yes, polished up, and covered in velvet the colour . . . the colour of old dried blood,' suggested David.

Luke looked at his watch. He should have been home ten minutes ago. *Murder in the Marsh* was over, so Anna-Louise's father would be expecting her home too.

But now the twins knew, Luke had no choice. He would have to let them in on the whole disaster.

'It *is* Mrs Harrington's chair . . .' he began.

With Delia and David's help, they carried the chair back to Luke's house in no time at all. All four crept round the side of the house to Luke's garden shed.

The shed was crammed with bags of potting compost, plant pots, garden chairs, Luke's mother's old bicycle. There was no space on the floor so they had to lift Mrs Harrington's chair and balance it in the wheelbarrow.

Luke and David gave Anna-Louise a hand-up over the fence so that she tumbled down on the dustbin on her side. She dusted herself down and slipped in the back door.

Just in time!

Anna-Louise's father drew up in his spotless green car with Anna-Louise's mother sitting beside him.

Luke and the twins ducked down behind the fence.

'Phew!' whispered David. 'That was close.'

'It's much more exciting at your house than our house,' said Delia with a grin.

Anna-Louise's mother got out of the passenger seat and opened the car boot.

'Henry, I want you to carry it,' she said. 'It's for her birthday and she mustn't see it. We'll put it in the shed for now.'

'Yes, dear,' said Anna-Louise's father.

Luke and the twins watched through a crack in the fence as a dainty little chair, painted white and gold with curvy legs was carried past by Anna-Louise's father.

'What do you think of the cover,

Henry? I finished it at the class tonight.'

The seat of the chair was a sickly yellow, sprinkled with little white daisies. Edging the seat was a wide frill of more of the daisy material, trimmed with dainty orange bows.

'It's very nice, dear.'

Anna-Louise's parents shut up the shed and disappeared through the shiny green door.

'Henry, don't forget to take off your shoes . . .' and the door shut behind them.

'Phew!' said Luke. 'We were just in time.'

'How are you going to get the hamster out?' said Delia.

'Oh, I'll come out in my pyjamas when I'm meant to be in bed.'

'Wow, that's exciting!' said David.

'And we'll get to school early tomorrow morning, just in case you need help with the chair.'

The twins slipped out the front gate and Luke retrieved his new Liverpool FC football. He was just dusting it down when he jumped at the sudden shriek of a super-powerful siren.

He dashed into his house and shut the door. Trembling, he ran up the stairs to his bedroom and peered round his curtains.

The police car screeched to a halt further up the road, beside the twins. Then David was pointing . . . in the direction of Luke and Anna-Louise's homes.

Why oh why had he ever thought he could trust the twins?

# 6. Police Questioning

The police car came slowly down the road, past Luke's house, and stopped . . . outside Anna-Louise's house.

The breath Luke had been holding in burst out in a sigh.

At least he was safe. But Anna-Louise could never keep a secret! She'd tell anyone everything if she was asked.

Luke sped downstairs, tiptoed out the

back door to the garden and crouched down by the crack in the fence. The police officer with the moustache was tapping sharply on the shiny green door while a second police officer, a very tall, thin lady, was peering through the window of Anna-Louise's tidy garden shed.

The shiny green door opened a crack.

'Good gracious, police!' came the shrill voice of Anna-Louise's mother. 'Anna-Louise is safe at home, so she can't have had an accident.'

The policeman with the moustache put his big black shoe on the step.

'You're not coming in with those shoes on,' said Anna-Louise's mother, surveying his shoe with horror.

'Just a few questions, madam. We believe you can help us with our enquiries.'

'What enquiries? And before you tell me, I would prefer it if you reversed your car up outside the house next door. What will the neighbours think if they see a police car outside our house?'

The policeman with the moustache ignored Anna-Louise's mother and

pulled out his notebook with a flourish. Behind him, the door of Anna-Louise's shed creaked open. The tall police lady had gone inside.

'So, madam, we believe you are interested in antique chairs?'

Anna-Louise's mother beamed at the policeman.

'I'm the best in the upholstery class at the Institute. I expect you're wanting a chair covered at Hopswood Police Station. You must have heard about me.'

'No, madam.' The policeman paused, and drew himself to attention. 'There has been a burglary at Hopswood Junior School.'

'No!'

'Yes, madam. We think it was perpetrated by someone who knew the school.'

'I don't know what this area is coming to. It was a respectable, quiet neighbourhood when we first came, but now,' Anna-Louise's mother leaned forward and whispered, ‘there are some noisy, rough boys in our street. Why don’t you go next door and try that boy Luke?’

Luke’s legs were beginning to ache with crouching down, but he didn’t dare move.

‘Madam, where were you between the hours of five and six o’clock this evening?’ persisted the policeman.

‘At my upholstery class. Why?’

‘Did you bring back a chair?’

‘Shush! It’s a surprise for my daughter,’ whispered Anna-Louise’s mother. ‘My husband, Henry, helped me bring it back in the car, didn’t you, Henry?’

‘Yes, dear,’ came a mumble from behind the green door.

Then the shed door banged back.

'PC Tollard.' It was a brisk woman's voice. 'It's here.'

The tall police lady strolled out holding the dinky white and gold chair in one hand.

'Put that down,' shrieked Anna-Louise's mother. 'You've got black gloves on. You'll mark the white paint.'

'We'll be taking that as evidence,' said the policeman, closing his book with a triumphant thump. 'We believe this chair to be stolen goods, stolen this evening from Hopswood Junior School between the hours of five and six o'clock, when you were out.'

'How absurd!' shrieked Anna-Louise's mother. 'Henry, do something about it. Stop this . . . it will kill me!'

Anna-Louise's father appeared blinking round the green door.

'I can't, dear.'

'And we would like you to accompany us to the police station for further questioning.'

Luke's heart had stopped beating. They were in a terrible muddle now.

The tall police lady helped Anna-Louise's mother, loudly protesting, into the back of the police car.

As the police car sped away Luke's heart started beating again. Anna-Louise's mother was lucky, really. What he would give to have a ride in a new police XK400 series B!

# 7. A Safe Recovery

Every night, Luke argued with his mother about his bedtime, but not tonight.

'Bedtime, Luke,' said his mother, at the end of the football highlights.

'Fine,' said Luke.

'Goodnight, son,' said Luke's father. 'I like your new responsible attitude.'

'I'll come up and tuck you in,' said Mum.

'No need, I'm going to read. I'll put my own light out.'

'The boy's growing up,' said Luke's father to his mother. 'We don't want to baby him.'

Luke changed into his pyjamas and lay on his bed and waited. He was afraid he'd drop off to sleep if he had to wait much longer. But then the noisy comedy show started and his mother's giggles and his father's chuckles drifted up through the ceiling below.

Luke crept down to the kitchen. He took the torch from the drawer by the back door, his lunch box with the holes, and a biscuit from the biscuit tin. Then he crept out to the garden shed.

The chair was stuck at an awkward angle on the wheelbarrow. He chose a big screwdriver from his father's toolbox and tried to prise out another brass tack.

It was impossible!

Could the hamster breathe in there?

Luke examined the chair. He couldn't spend all night getting the hamster out.

There was only one thing to do.

With the screwdriver, he made a small hole in the velvet at the edge of the seat. He put two fingers in and ripped the fabric back. He plunged his hand into the seat stuffing and felt something warm, and soft, with sharp teeth.

'Ow!' Luke yelled as he pulled the hamster out.

He popped the hamster into his lunch box, together with the biscuit. At least the hamster could breathe in there. Luke had made holes in it when he'd had to rescue the hamster once before.

He then pulled down their holiday tent, which lay neatly folded on a shelf, and draped it over the chair. His father only went into the shed at weekends and, if anyone looked in through the window, all they would see was a mound of green canvas.

Luke grabbed his lunch box, shut the door quietly, and tiptoed back up the stairs to bed.

'Luke, I can't find your lunch box,' said Luke's mother at breakfast the following morning. 'You must have left it at school.'

'Mmm,' said Luke, munching his toast.

'Strange though,' said Mum. 'I could have sworn I washed it out last night. You'll have to take your sandwiches in a plastic bag.'

After breakfast Luke went round to Anna-Louise's house and rang the ding-dong chiming bell, next to the

'NO HAWKERS, NO VENDORS, NO CANVASSERS, NO CALLERS WITHOUT APPOINTMENT' sign. The door was opened at once by Anna-Louise, holding a finger to her lips.

'Sh! We're not allowed to say a word or make a sound. Mummy says she'll die if there's any noise or anyone speaks to her.'

'She's all right then?' said Luke with relief. 'I saw her go off in the police car.'

'The police asked her questions at the police station, then they brought her home. They wouldn't let her bring back that chair she was working on at her upholstery class. She says it's a *disgrace* and a *scandal* and that she is going to write to the *Hopswood News*. What are we going to do about the hamster, Luke?'

Luke held up his lunch box with the holes.

'He's in here!'

'You're brilliant, Luke.' Luke felt himself grow at least two centimetres with pride. 'But we'll have to take the chair too, won't we?'

'Can't,' explained Luke. 'I've ripped the plum velvet off. It's got stuffing hanging out now and the inspectors won't like that.'

'But there'll be trouble, Luke.' Anna-Louise's voice trembled. 'What will Mrs Harrington sit on in assembly?'

'She'll have to stand.'

# 8. Creak! Crack!

Everyone was talking in Class 3 of Hopswood Junior School.

'Have you heard about the burglary yesterday?' said Ali to Luke.

'Uhmm . . .'

'They had a police car up here, a new XK400 series B, and they stole Mrs Harrington's chair.'

'Mr Pigott! Mr Pigott!' called

Samantha breathlessly. 'I think they stole the hamster too. I was first in the classroom and I looked for him . . .'

Everybody turned towards the hamster's cage at the back of the classroom. Anna-Louise stood beside the cage, Luke's lunch box in her hand, her face as glowing as her ginger curls.

Delia pushed Anna-Louise aside and opened the cage.

'The hamster's here,' she said. 'You didn't look very thoroughly, did you, Samantha?'

'But I *did* look. I searched everywhere,' said Samantha indignantly.

Mr Pigott was admiring himself in the wall mirror by the door. His hair had been cut and his beard was clipped into a little point.

'Well done, Class 3,' he said. 'We are

ready for the inspectors. The classroom is neat and tidy and now we will line up *quietly* to go in to assembly.'

'What's Mrs Harrington going to sit on without her big chair?' said Ali.

'She can sit on a PE mat,' said Samantha. 'There are plenty of PE mats in the hall.'

'We have to sit on the floor,' said Ali. 'Why can't she sit on the floor like us?'

'Hush!' said Mr Pigott grinning, his big teeth brilliant in his neatly trimmed beard. 'The Hopswood Police have come to our rescue. The chair was found last night at the home of some known criminal. When they heard we had inspectors visiting today, they promised to return it in time for assembly.'

*

The inspectors were already seated on the platform when Class 3 filed in to assembly. There were two of them. One was a man with snow-white hair and twinkly eyes, who beamed down at the children. The other was a lady with long, dark hair and a floaty dress.

Anna-Louise nudged Luke.

'They're not in raincoats,' she whispered. 'Where does she keep her handcuffs? That floaty dress doesn't have any pockets.'

'Handcuffs? Don't be daft, Anna-Louise,' muttered Luke.

There was a loud hiss. Luke looked up to meet the steely glare of Mr Pigott.

'Mrs Harrington's chair isn't back,' Anna-Louise whispered again.

'Of course it's not back,' muttered

Luke angrily. 'It's under the tent in our shed. Shush!'

The door from Mrs Harrington's study had opened. Just as she walked out in her best grey suit there was a loud knocking at the door that led in from the playground. The door swung open, and in came the police inspector with the moustache. In one hand he carried a tiny white and gold chair, with a sickly yellow, daisy sprinkled, orange bowed seat.

For once Mrs Harrington seemed to have nothing to say.

'Just in time,' said the policeman, grinning. 'We made a special effort. We know what an important day it is for Hopswood School.' He nodded towards the inspectors who were watching with interest.

'But . . .' Mrs Harrington spluttered.

'All solved,' said the policeman. 'We like to clear up crime quickly in Hopswood. I'll slip out quietly and leave you to get on with assembly.'

The policeman clattered out of the hall in his big black shoes.

The children stared in astonishment. For the first time ever there was not a cough, a whisper or a scuffle in assembly.

'Well.' Mrs Harrington drew in a deep breath. 'Good morning, everyone, and a special welcome to . . .'

No one listened. All eyes were on the tiny chair.

'. . . and now, children, we will sit down to hear Class 2's poems about rain.'

The children flopped like rag dolls to

the floor, all eyes forward, staring intently at Mrs Harrington.

Gingerly, she sat down. The little chair creaked and swayed. Mrs Harrington's bottom was too big for the tiny chair.

The inspectors listened with interest to three children from Class 2 who read their poems in turn. Luke didn't hear a word. His worried ears were straining to hear the creaks of the chair.

> '*The rain drops down in winter*
> *And on the pavement glitters . . .*'

*Crack!* A white and gold leg slid sideways from under the chair. Mrs Harrington slid with a bump to the floor.

Luke screwed up his eyes. He didn't dare look any more. The sight on the

platform was too terrible.

When he opened them again, the man with snow-white hair was giving his arm to Mrs Harrington to help her up from the floor, and the lady with the floaty dress was picking up Mrs Harrington's big black handbag.

Grim-faced, Mr Pigott marched Class 3 out of assembly.

Luke felt a tug on his arm.

'We'll all go to prison, won't we?' said Anna-Louise.

'Don't be stupid, Anna-Louise.'

'But the school will never pass the inspection now, will it?'

## 9. 'Don't Put Me in Prison'

'It's all your fault,' said Luke furiously to David and Delia.

Mr Pigott had put Luke, the twins and Anna-Louise together on a table at the back of the classroom, to write up their journals.

'You saw Anna-Louise's father carry in that silly chair and you told the policemen to look for the stolen chair in

Anna-Louise's shed.'

'Now Mummy will go to prison,' said Anna-Louise, chewing her pencil. 'And if the inspectors don't like my story, I'll have to go with her too.'

David and Delia sat blinking their big blue eyes and smiling.

'You should be grovelling at our feet,' said Delia. 'You wouldn't have got the hamster out if they had taken Mrs Harrington's chair.'

'You'd have been in big trouble, Luke,' agreed David. 'Storing stolen goods.'

Mr Pigott looked up from his desk at the front.

'What is all that talking on Luke's table? David and Delia, are Luke and Anna-Louise distracting you again?'

Luke sucked his pencil and then

began a story about an XK400 series B police car, with the latest roof-mounted search lights and a super-powerful siren.

Delia described how a lady with long, dark hair and a floaty dress was riding over a bridge on her bike when she was dragged off, and thrown head first into the sinking mud of the marsh below.

David wrote about a man with white hair and sparkly eyes who, after struggling bravely, was tipped out of a boat on the marsh into muddy, squishy depths below.

Anna-Louise stared in panic at her blank piece of paper.

The door into the classroom opened quietly and the lady in the floaty dress with long dark hair slipped into the classroom.

She held up her hand to Mr Pigott

who was trying to twist his mouth into a smile.

'Please don't take any notice of me,' said the lady inspector. 'I can see the children are busy. I'll just wander around and look at what they are writing.'

Slowly, the inspector moved among the tables, stopping here and there to read what a child had written.

Anna-Louise sat rigid, staring at her empty piece of paper. The lady was almost at their table.

Then Anna-Louise grabbed her chewed and soggy pencil and wrote a line.

The lady stopped behind the twins.

'What a lot you've both written,' she smiled, but as she read their diaries her smile faded.

She looked at Luke's long list of police car facts and figures and nodded.

Then she stopped behind Anna-Louise.

'PLEASE DON'T PUT ME IN PRISON!' she read aloud. 'What an exciting opening to your story. Who is meant to be saying that? No, don't tell me. You go on and write the story. I can see it's going to be very original.'

Mr Pigott stared at Anna-Louise with astonishment.

As school ended, David and Delia hung around the classroom chatting to Mr Pigott about what fun inspections were, how nice Mr Pigott's beard looked, and how lively the hamster was.

Meanwhile, Luke and Anna-Louise hurried out to the dustbins at the back of the school.

Sticking out of one large dustbin was a flounce of daisy material and a white spindly chair leg.

Luke hauled himself up, scraped off a pile of crisp bags, cola cans and wet tea bags, and pulled out what remained of Anna-Louise's mother's chair.

'It's missing a leg,' wailed Anna-Louise. 'It won't stand up without four legs.'

Luke shinned up the side of the big dustbin again and peered in. He couldn't see a white and gold chair leg, and he didn't like the look of all that dirty rubbish below.

'If I jump into the bin, it will be like sinking mud. I'll disappear under a stinking mound of rubbish and you'll probably never see me again.'

'Oh, don't do that,' said Anna-Louise anxiously. 'I don't know why Mummy's chair has been thrown in the rubbish bin. She'll die if she hears Mr Tump thought her chair was rubbish.'

'Anyway,' said Luke cheerfully, 'some stools have three legs, don't they?'

# 10. A Chair with a Difference

It wasn't difficult getting the little chair back to Anna-Louise's house. It was so light that Luke and Anna-Louise took it in turns to carry it. They slipped down the path to Anna-Louise's garden shed and tried to stand the chair in the middle of the floor.

'It doesn't work with three legs,' wailed Anna-Louise, as the chair collapsed on its side for the second time.

Luke searched round the shed. Standing in a corner was a silver coal bucket full of barbecue briquettes.

'That'll do,' said Luke quickly, as he emptied the briquettes out on the floor. 'The bucket is almost the same height as the chair legs.'

They were propping the corner of the seat on the upturned silver bucket when they heard the green door open.

'Is that you back, Anna-Louise?' came a muffled squawk. 'Come in and shut the door.'

'Yes, Mummy,' said Anna-Louise, running out of the shed.

'The shame of it!' went on the voice from behind the door. 'Police calling at our house! What's that black dust all over your shoes? It looks very like coal dust to me. Get those shoes off at once!'

When Luke heard the door slam shut, he crunched out across the coal briquettes, climbed on the dustbins, shinned over the fence and leaped down into his own back garden.

After tea, Anna-Louise's mother announced to her daughter, 'I'm watching television now. It's *Gardener's Delight* with Angus Throttlebush. You'd better do your homework upstairs.'

'Yes, Mummy.'

Next door, Luke's mother was examining the *TV Times*.

'I know you were disappointed about *Murder in the Marsh* yesterday, Luke, and you were so good about it. If you've done your homework, why don't you watch *Mars Explorer*? It says here, "an exciting space adventure".'

'Actually, I thought I'd go out to the shed and do a bit of woodwork.'

His mother lowered the *TV Times* with surprise.

'Woodwork? How I used to love woodwork when I was a boy!' said Luke's father. 'Magazine racks, shelves, useful boxes – I made them all. Yes! There's nothing like an interesting hobby to beat television.'

Luke's mother looked at Luke suspiciously. As he closed the kitchen door she said, 'Do you think Luke's all right?'

David and Delia's mother was delighted.

'Playing at Luke's house. Now that's a

nice friend for you. He's such a good quiet boy.'

In the cluttered shed, Luke pulled away the green tent covering Mrs Harrington's chair. Anna-Louise, David and Delia stared at it in horror.

'It looks terrible,' said David.

'The stuffing is all coming out,' said Delia.

'The lovely plum velvet cover is ruined!' cried Anna-Louise, fingering the velvet shreds.

Luke turned to them crossly.

'How did you think I was going to get the hamster out? I had to rip off the velvet. Now listen, this is what we'll have to do. Each of us will take a side of the chair seat and nail the new cover down.'

'What are we going to cover with seat with?' demanded Delia.

'I've thought about that too,' said Luke. 'Anna-Louise's mother wears a clean apron every day. She's got hundreds of aprons. If Anna-Louise borrows one, we can cut out a big piece for the chair. She'll never notice.'

'She will,' said Anna-Louise.

'Luke, why don't you cut down your mum's kitchen curtains,' suggested Delia.

'No,' said Luke.

Then a horrible idea popped into his head.

'There's my football banner, pinned to my bedroom wall,' he groaned.

Anna-Louise gasped. 'The special banner your uncle in Liverpool sent?'

*

It didn't take long to cut up the football banner. With all four of them working at once, they banged the brass tacks in with a hammer, a broken barbecue briquette, a gardening trowel and an old shoe that Luke's grandpa's dog liked to chase.

Mrs Harrington's chair certainly looked different. It had a red seat with a yellow crest and LIVERPOOL FC in big yellow letters across the middle.

'Unusual,' said Delia, standing back to admire her work.

'Original,' agreed David.

'What a waste!' groaned Luke.

'I liked the plum velvet best,' sighed Anna-Louise.

They lifted the chair back into the wheelbarrow and covered it up again with the green tent.

Three figures crept out into the night. The fourth was so exhausted that he fell into bed with his shoes on.

'Look at that!' said Luke's mother, as she pulled off his trainers. 'Who said he was too grown up to have his mum tuck him up?'

# 11. Who Supports Liverpool?

Anna-Louise arrived on Luke's doorstep early in the morning.

'You're very early, Anna-Louise,' said Luke's mother. 'How's school going?' Luke pushed past his mother at the door. 'What's the hurry, Luke?'

'Got to be there early,' Luke muttered. Then he called back to his father, 'Dad, could I take the wheelbarrow to school?

I'll bring it back tonight.'

'Working in the school garden again, are you?' called his father. 'Hold on. I'll come out and give you a hand. There's a lot of stuff in that shed.'

Anna-Louise stared in panic at Luke.

'No, Dad. Anna-Louise is helping me. You finish your breakfast.'

In the kitchen, Luke's parents poured out their second cup of coffee.

'I like the way that boy is shaping up,' said his father. 'He's more thoughtful and considerate.'

'I don't know,' murmured Luke's mother. 'Anna-Louise, poor scrap, looked frightened out of her mind.'

Luke and Anna-Louise each took a handle of the wheelbarrow and wobbled along the road to school. The huge mound in the wheelbarrow was hidden by the green tent.

David and Delia were waiting outside the school gates. Luke fished in his pocket for the key and unlocked the gates.

'Get in quick,' said David. 'Mr Tump is carrying in the parcels and letters to the school secretary's office.'

Delia held the gate open and Luke and Anna-Louise wobbled over with the wheelbarrow to Mr Tump's house. All four children lifted the chair down and set it in Mr Tump's workshop. Luke hung the key back on the board.

Mr Tump limped out of the school secretary's office and into the playground.

'Heh! Stop there!' he shouted, pushing his glasses up his nose. 'How did you lot get in this early? The gates aren't open yet. And what's that you've got there?'

'We're going to weed the school garden,' said Delia, smiling, and blinking her big blue eyes.

Mr Tump scratched his head.

'Don't make no sense to me. You should have weeded the garden *before* the inspectors came, not afterwards.'

*

Mrs Harrington stood up straight in assembly in her second-best brown suit.

'Well done, children! I have glimpsed the draft report, and the inspectors praise the impressive concentration and outstanding attention by everyone in assembly.'

The children began to clap. Mrs Harrington held up her hand for quiet.

'And more good news. Mr Tump has found my chair . . .'

'Mrs Harrington,' Mr Tump called from the side.

'. . . which I believe is magnificently renovated,' went on Mrs Harrington, who didn't like being interrupted.

'Mrs Harrington!' Mr Tump waved his hands above his head.

Mrs Harrington frowned. 'Sit down,

children. Now we will listen to Class One's readings on sunshine.'

The children slumped to the floor. But Mrs Harrington didn't sit. She stood staring down at her chair.

'Mr Tump,' her voice echoed icily, 'what is the meaning of this extraordinary . . . Liverpool FC seat covering?'

'I had a lovely bit of plum velvet on the seat, Mrs Harrington, but the burglars . . .'

Back in Class Three, Mr Pigott stroked his beard thoughtfully.

'Luke, you're the only supporter of Liverpool FC I know of.'

'Yes,' said Anna-Louise. 'Luke's uncle lives in Liver . . . Ow! David and Delia are standing on my toes!'

'Luke's not a Liverpool supporter,' said David, grinning. 'It's Manchester United that's your team, isn't it, Luke?'

'Manchester United,' agreed Luke, crossing his fingers behind his back. 'Yeah, that's my team.'

Luke was furious as he sat down to write his journal. To think that he had disowned his team for the sake of Anna-Louise!

'I'll make you a new banner,' came a small voice beside him.

'I'm not going to speak to you ever again,' muttered Luke.

'But I'm much better at sewing than

writing stories. I'll make you a big banner to go right across your wall.'

'You couldn't,' said Luke doubtfully. 'You'd need a big piece of red material.'

'I know where Mummy keeps her old dust sheets. I'll dye one red.'

'Your mother would never let you,' said Luke. 'It would make an awful mess.'

'We could go to your house,' suggested Anna-Louise. 'I could walk back with you.'

Luke chewed his pencil and thought.

'I bet Mum would help us,' he said enthusiastically. 'You'd better come home with me this afternoon and you can tell her what we'll need.'

'Yes,' said Anna-Louise happily. 'That would be lovely. I've got lots of time now I'm not going to prison.'